red sled

by LITA JUDGE

Atheneum Books for Young Readers

New York · London · Toronto · Sydney

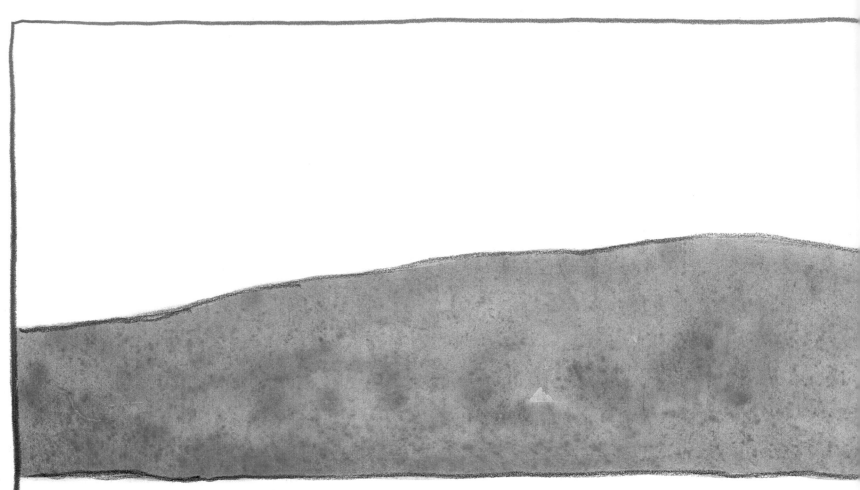

For Dave

ATHENEUM BOOKS FOR YOUNG READERS

An imprint of Simon & Schuster Children's Publishing Division

1230 Avenue of the Americas, New York, New York 10020

Copyright © 2011 by Lita Judge

All rights reserved, including the right of reproduction in whole or in part in any form.

ATHENEUM BOOKS FOR YOUNG READERS is a registered trademark of Simon & Schuster, Inc.

For information about special discounts for bulk purchases, please contact Simon & Schuster Special Sales

at 1-866-506-1949 or business@simonandschuster.com.

The Simon & Schuster Speakers Bureau can bring authors to your live event. For more information or to

book an event, contact the Simon & Schuster Speakers Bureau at 1-866-248-3049 or visit our website

at www.simonspeakers.com.

Book design by Ann Bobco

The text for this book is set in Fairfield LH and Bodoni Oldface.

The illustrations for this book are rendered in pencil and watercolor.

Manufactured in China

0811 SCP

First Edition

10 9 8 7 6 5 4 3 2 1

Library of Congress Cataloging-in-Publication Data

Judge, Lita.

Red sled / Lita Judge. —1st ed.

p. cm.

Summary: At night, a host of woodland creatures plays with a child's red sled.

ISBN 978-1-4424-2007-6 (hardcover)

ISBN 978-1-4424-3552-0 (eBook)

[1. Sleds—Fiction. 2. Forest animals—Fiction. 3. Sounds, Words for—Fiction.] I. Title.

PZ7.J894Red 2011

[E]—dc22

2010033264

Scrinch scrunch scrinch scrunch scrinch scrunch

Scrunch scrinch scrunch scrinch scrunch scrinch

eeeeeeece

oooooo eoeoeoee

Alley-oop

Gadung Gadung

Gadung

Gadung

ssssssffft

Scrinch scrunch scrinch scrunch scrinch scrunch

The End